Mar 19

Kylie Jean

Gymnastics Queen

by Marci Peschke

illustrated by Tuesday Mourning

PICTURE WINDOW BOOKS
a capstone imprint

Kylie Jean is published by Picture Window Books
A Capstone Imprint
1710 Roe Crest Drive
North Mankato, Minnesota 56003
www.mycapstone.com

Library of Congress Cataloging-in-Publication Data
Names: Peschke, M. (Marci), author. Mourning, Tuesday, illustrator.
Peschke, M. (Marci) Kylie Jean.
Title: Gymnastics queen / by Marci Peschke ; illustrated by Tuesday Mourning.
Description: North Mankato, Minnesota : Picture Window Books, a Capstone imprint. [2017]
Series: Kylie Jean | Summary: The Summer Olympics inspires Kylie Jean Carter to take gymnastics lessons, but even better than that is making a new friend, Abby, who is deaf, and starting to learn sign language.
Identifiers: LCCN 2015050697|
ISBN 978-1-5158-0052-1 (library binding)
ISBN 978-1-5158-0053-8 (paper over board)
ISBN 978-1-5158-0054-5 (ebook pdf)
Subjects: LCSH: Artistic gymnastics—Juvenile fiction. | Deaf children—Juvenile fiction.
Friendship—Juvenile fiction. Families—Texas—Juvenile fiction. Texas—Juvenile fiction.
CYAC: Gymnastics—Fiction. Deaf—Fiction. People with disabilities—Fiction. Friendship—Fiction.
Family life—Texas—Fiction. Texas—Fiction.
Classification: LCC PZ7.P441245 Gy 2017 | DDC 813.6—dc23
LC record available at http://lccn.loc.gov/2015050697

Creative Director: *Nathan Gassman*
Graphic Designer: *Sarah Bennett*
Editor: *Shelly Lyons*
Production Specialist: *Kathy McColley*

Design Element Credit:
Shutterstock/blue67design

Printed and bound in China.
000374

For Marissa and all of my SUPER fans!
—MP

Table of Contents

All About Me, Kylie Jean!

My name is Kylie Jean Carter. I live in a big, sunny, yellow house on Peachtree Lane in Jacksonville, Texas, with Momma, Daddy, and my two brothers, T.J. and Ugly Brother.

T.J. is my older brother, and Ugly Brother is . . . well . . . he's really a dog. Don't you go telling him he is a dog. Okay? I mean it. He thinks he is a real, true person.

He is a black-and-white bulldog. His front looks like his back, all smashed in. His face is all droopy like he's sad, but he's not.

His two front teeth stick out, and his tongue hangs down. (Now you know why his name is Ugly Brother.)

Everyone I love to the moon and back lives in Jacksonville. Nanny, Pa, Granny, Pappy, my aunts, my uncles, and my cousins all live here. I'm extra lucky, because I can see all of them any time I want to!

My momma says I'm pretty. She says I have eyes as blue as the summer sky and a smile as sweet as an angel. (Momma says pretty is as pretty does. That means being nice to the old folks, taking care of little animals, and respecting my momma and daddy.)

But I'm pretty on the outside and on the inside. My hair is long, brown, and curly.

I wear it in a ponytail sometimes, but my absolute most favorite is when Momma pulls it back in a princess style on special days.

I just gave you a little hint about my big dream. Ever since I was a bitty baby I have wanted to be an honest-to-goodness beauty queen. I even know the wave. It's side to side, nice and slow, with a dazzling smile. I practice all the time, because everybody knows beauty queens need to have a perfect wave.

I'm Kylie Jean, and I'm going to be a beauty queen. Just you wait and see!

Chapter One
Tumbling Gold

It's afternoon, and I'm lying on my bed, staring at my ceiling again. Outside it is hotter than a firecracker in July! I swear, Momma could fry some eggs right on our front walkway. Yup, it's summer in Texas, all right!

Mr. Weather Man says that we have had fifty straight days over one hundred degrees. I'm hot and bored. Momma wants me to stay inside unless it is early in the morning or late at night. That's when it finally cools down a tiny bit.

I'm trying to find things to do inside. In my room, the air conditioner blows all day long. By dinnertime it's as worn out as a lawn mower on the last day of summer.

I call my best cousin, Lucy, on the phone. Then I remember she's gone away on vacation to see her grandparents. I sigh. Ugly Brother looks at me with his sad old puppy dog eyes.

"We've just got to find something to do!" I say.

"Ruff, ruff!" he barks.

Two barks mean yes, and one bark means no. He's hot, too. His slimy pink tongue is hangin' out and so much drool is drippin' down, it looks like a shower. We sit on the floor by my fluffy, pink bed. Thinking of something to do is really hard!

We've already done everything there is to do inside. We've been in the house every day since school got out!

"Do you want to put together a puzzle or read a book?" I ask.

"Ruff!"

Come to think of it, a puzzle is not a good idea after all. "You always get the puzzle pieces all slimy with doggie drool," I say.

Then I suggest we color or paint. I love art and am famous for my sunflower paintings. I've painted sunflowers for Granny, Nanny, and Miss Clarabelle. But it's clear Ugly Brother doesn't want to paint. He's sitting on my art tablet, so I can't even reach my supplies. I guess I'm out of ideas!

I am lying on my bed again when I hear Momma cheering and shouting. My curiosity gets the best of me, so I slip downstairs to see what in the world is going on. In the living room, Momma has the Summer Olympics on TV. Swimmers in a giant pool move back and forth, back and forth. Watching them for even a minute is boring! Besides, I'm a teeny, tiny bit jealous of them being in that nice cool pool.

Momma sees us standing by the door. "Hey, sugar, what are you two up to?" she asks.

"We're so bored! We tried to think of something to do, but there's nothing!" I reply.

"Why don't you watch the Olympics with me for a while?" Momma offers. "I can make us a little snack."

I am not interested in watching the Olympics, but Ugly Brother's ears stand up as soon as Momma says the word *snack*. I hesitate, but Ugly Brother starts to whimper and beg. He is *always* hungry.

"Okay," I say.

Momma heads for the kitchen. "This is going to be fun!" she promises.

Soon I hear *POP, POP, POP*. It's the sweet sound of popcorn! Maybe watching swimming won't be so bad. Momma comes back with a giant bowl of salty, buttery popcorn and two icy bottles of Coke.

We snuggle into the cushions, and I toss Ugly Brother a piece of popcorn. He catches it on his slimy tongue.

When the commercials are finally over, there's no swimming pool. Guess what? Gymnastics is on next! Momma, Ugly Brother, and I watch and munch.

"The good ol' U.S.A. is in the lead!" I shout.

"I know. I like Courtney Bell. She's the star gymnast for Team U.S.A.," says Momma.

First, Courtney does an exercise on something called a balance beam.

Momma explains, "A balance beam is a long narrow block of wood that the gymnast performs on. She has to be able to go forward, backward, flip, and turn without losing her balance."

We watch. Courtney is so good! Pointing her toes, she twists and turns. She never slips or slides like she's going to fall. No wonder she's Team U.S.A.'s number-one girl! When she gets to the end, she jumps down and spreads her arms like a swan's wings. She is so beautiful and graceful. I think I might just have a new inspiration.

Team U.S.A. moves on to the floor exercise. That's even more fun to watch than the balance beam. In between each gymnast, I give Ugly Brother some popcorn so he won't get bored. I'm having fun, and I want him to have fun too.

"Who chooses their music?" I ask.

Momma tells me that each gymnast picks out her own music and then choreographs her gymnastics moves to go with it, almost like a dance.

We cheer and cheer at the end of each routine, and so do the fans in the stands. Our gymnasts are wearing red, white, and blue leotards. The leotards look like bathing suits with long sleeves.

Next up are the Russian gymnasts, and then China's team performs.

"Yay!" I shout. "The U.S.A. is still the best!"

Momma says, "I think you're favoring the U.S.A. But they are our team, after all!"

Ugly Brother and I both eat some more popcorn while we wait for the final scores. Ugly Brother can't do gymnastics, but we show Momma his new trick. I toss the popcorn in the air, and he jumps off the couch and catches it on his tongue.

Momma is impressed and cheers for him. He is so proud that he runs in a circle and chases his tail. Maybe he could learn some gymnastics — and maybe I could, too!

That's when an idea starts turning in my brain like a gymnast on a beam. I need to take some gymnastics lessons! I know a move or two, but I have a feeling I need to learn a lot more.

Finally, they are ready to announce the medal winners. Watching the Olympics with Momma and Ugly Brother has actually been fun. I can hardly wait to see who will win the gold.

Guess what? It's our favorite gymnast, Courtney Bell! Hip, hip, hooray!

Chapter Two
A Pup, a Flip, and a Pal

Early the next morning, Momma suggests I take Ugly Brother for a walk to the park.

Ugly Brother is full of energy after being cooped up inside with me. When he hears Momma say the word *park*, he runs to get his leash.

"Don't stay out too long," warns Momma. "And make sure you wear sunscreen. That Texas sun will you give you a sunburn morning, noon, or night!"

I laugh because Momma is teasing me about the night part. Everyone knows you can't get sunburn at night. "Yes, ma'am. I've got sunscreen and water. I promise I won't stay long."

"I love you, Sweet Pea," says Momma.

"Bye!"

The back screen door slams as Ugly Brother pulls me down the driveway.

"Hey! Slow down," I yell.

"Ruff!" he barks.

He is ready to run. Pecan Park is only a few blocks from our house, but I am out of breath when we get there. I hold on to Ugly Brother's leash with all my might. I can feel the leather strap cutting into my hand.

"STOP!" I command.

He is not listening. Something has his attention, and the leash is slipping out of my sweaty hand. He breaks free, finally getting away from me. He runs and runs until I can't see him anymore.

I do NOT want to tell Momma I've lost my dog brother, so I've got to find him! The park is gigantic. I look around, but I don't see him anywhere. Maybe he's cooling off down by the creek. That would be a nice cool spot. I head down the grassy slope to check. I see tall grassy reeds and dragonflies. I hear bees and frogs, but no dogs. He's not here!

I'm getting nervous! I call and call him, but he doesn't come. I wonder if he could be in my favorite spot at the park — the playground!

When I get to the playground, I see my friend Paula Dupree, but not my naughty doggy brother. I wave at Paula, and I keep looking for Ugly Brother. Then I finally see him. He is playing with the cutest little black pup.

I call, "Ugly Brother! Ugly Brother!"

Some of the people in the park turn to look when they hear me calling. But Ugly Brother is too busy playing with his new friend to pay attention.

As I'm walking across the field, I see a girl doing a back handspring. She lands it perfectly. Then she turns and signs to a lady near her.

Just then, an idea dances across my brain like a gymnast doing a floor exercise. I could be a tumbling queen just like Courtney Bell! First, I need to find out how that girl learned to do those back handsprings. I head over to her right away.

"Hello, my name is Kylie Jean Carter," I announce, "and that's my dog, Ugly Brother." I point to my dog.

The girl doesn't respond. Her back is to me. At first, I think she must be really rude.

Her momma speaks up. "Hello, Kylie. I'm Tonya Golden, and that's my daughter, Abby. She's deaf, so she can't hear us speak. Abby speaks sign language and reads lips."

"Oh!" I say. "Can you tell her I say *hello*?"

"Of course," says Mrs. Golden. "Ugly Brother is a very unusual name for a dog. We named our little black dog Domino."

Mrs. Golden signs our conversation for Abby. She looks puzzled.

Laughing, I say, "He has another name. It's Bruno, but he likes Ugly Brother better. And I like Kylie Jean."

Mrs. Golden nods. "I see."

"Can you tell me where Abby learned to tumble like that?" I ask.

Mrs. Golden signs to Abby. I can tell Abby has a lot to say. Mrs. Golden tells me that Abby wants me to know all about the Gold Star Gymnastics Center where she takes lessons.

Mrs. Golden explains, "They are getting ready for a really big showcase event right now, and it's going to be exciting!"

Wow, that sounds amazing! "Can anyone take lessons at the gymnastics center?" I ask. "And can you teach me how to say *hi* in sign language?"

A huge smile crosses Abby's momma's face. "Yes, and yes!" she says.

She tells me to watch and then motions like a military salute. Abby laughs and salutes her mother. Then I salute Abby. We all laugh. Saying *hello* in sign language is fun and easy. I have made a new friend! Plus she has an adorable little dog who is Ugly Brother's new friend!

Grabbing the leash, I decide to say good-bye. I wave to my new friend, and then I turn away. I need to take Ugly Brother home before he runs off again. I am so excited that I drag him all the way home, just like he dragged me to the park earlier.

Momma is waiting for me in the kitchen. "It's starting to get hot," she says. "I was getting a little worried. What took you so long at the park, sugar?"

"I want to take gymnastics lessons," I blurt out. "I met a new friend named Abby. She's a gymnast. Ugly Brother met a new doggy friend, too. His name is Domino, and he is a tiny black dog."

Momma laughs. "Wow, that's great news. It sounds like you've had quite an adventure!"

Hello, I sign to Momma, making a quick salute. I add, "Abby is deaf, and I just learned how to say *hello* in sign language."

Momma hands me one of her delicious homemade strawberry watermelon ice pops. It's the perfect treat on such a hot day! I tell her all about our adventure at the park, and I explain that I want to be a gymnastics queen. Then I tell her about the Gold Star Gymnastics Center.

"I know just where that place is," Momma tells me. "It's right down Little Creek Road."

"Can I take lessons there?" I ask. "Pretty please with sugar on top? If you say yes, I will help out around the house and do extra chores! You know I'm a good helper, too!"

Momma licks her yummy ice pop. She tells me to finish mine, and then we'll look on the computer to find out about the lessons and the showcase. I bite my ice pop instead of licking. I can't wait to sign up for lessons! After all, I am a soon-to-be gymnastics queen.

Chapter Three
Going to Gold Star

On Monday morning, as soon as the pale yellow sun chases away the silvery moon, I slip downstairs. It's early, but I have been counting down the minutes ever since Saturday, when Momma agreed to take me to the gymnastics center. Today is sign-up day. I am so excited! Maybe I will see Abby there.

I decide to wake up Momma with breakfast in bed as a thank-you for letting me take lessons.

First, I get a pretty tray out of the cabinet. Then
I rinse some fresh strawberries, put them in a little
red bowl, and sprinkle some sugar on top. There
are some leftover pancakes in the freezer, so I pull
them out and pop them in the microwave. Then
I place a pat of butter and some maple syrup on
top. Last, I pour Momma's favorite orange juice
in the glass with red cherries painted on it. Ugly
Brother comes in and sits by the stove.

"Are you here to help?" I ask.

He barks, "Ruff, ruff."

He can't help much, so I tell him to keep me
company. When everything is ready, I put it on
the tray with a pretty pink lace napkin and some
silverware.

"I wish I could make Momma coffee, but I'm not old enough yet," I say. "It's okay, though. This breakfast sure looks tasty."

Again he barks, "Ruff, ruff."

"I'm taking this up to Momma," I tell him. "You stay out of my way, okay?"

He sits down, and I head upstairs. Daddy has already gone to work. I set down the tray and tip-tap knock on the door.

"Come in," Momma says sleepily from inside.

I open the door, pick up the tray, and carry it to the bed. When Momma sees it, her eyes light up like fireflies.

"For me?" she asks.

"Yes, ma'am!" I reply.

"What a treat!" Momma exclaims. "This breakfast tray is pretty as a picture! And just what did I do to deserve being treated like a queen today?"

"I wanted to do something special for you, Momma," I say. "Especially since you agreed to let me take gymnastics lessons."

Momma smiles. "Well just remember that you also promised to do extra chores," she says. "I also think some of the lesson fees should come from your piggy bank."

"Yes, ma'am. I will help pay, Momma," I say.

After breakfast, we get ready to go. I get dressed, brush my teeth, and head toward the door. As I step outside, Ugly Brother darts through the door and jumps into the van!

"Sorry, Ugly Brother," I say, "but gymnastics isn't for doggies!"

He makes the saddest little doggie face as I start leading him back into the house.

Momma crosses her arms. "Sorry, Ugly Brother," she says. "NO dogs allowed today!"

As we drive, visions of gymnasts tumble in my head. "Please hurry, Momma!" I beg.

"Hold your horses, sugar!" Momma replies. "Little Creek Road is not too far. It's just down Main Street and a few turns past the school."

The sun is brighter now, glinting like a gold medal in the sky as we pull into the parking lot.

"I think the Olympics must be inspiring a lot of girls," Momma says. "The parking lot is full!"

The building looks sort of like Pa's big metal horse training barn, except it's painted a really pretty sunflower gold color. Large windows run down one side, and there is a big gold star near the front door.

Inside, we see girls tumbling, swinging, and practicing with coaches. I see a tiny girl with red hair waving and smiling. It's Abby Golden! She must be taking lessons today. I sign *hello*.

"Momma, that girl is my new friend from the park," I explain.

Momma smiles and salutes hello, too.

We go to the welcome desk, and a nice lady gives us several forms to complete. We sit at a little table and fill out all of them.

After we're finished, we get to take a tour of the facility. It has a big floor mat, uneven bars, a balance beam, and something called a horse, but it doesn't actually look like a real horse. I can start classes with the beginner group tomorrow.

Momma and I go watch Abby. She dismounts from the bars with a twist. Then she waves at us again and smiles. As I'm waving back, I see Abby's mom on the other side of the mat.

"Come on, Momma!" I say. "I have someone I want you to meet."

I grab Momma's hand and pull her in the direction of Abby's mom. We walk over the squishy mats in our stocking feet until we are standing right in front of Mrs. Golden.

"This is Mrs. Golden, Abby's mother," I say in my politest voice. "Mrs. Golden, this is Mrs. Carter, my mother."

"You can call me Tonya," Mrs. Golden says, smiling widely.

"And you can call me Shelley," says Momma.

The mommas chat while I watch Abby practice. When it's time to go, I ask Mrs. Golden to tell Abby I will see her tomorrow. Mrs. Golden teaches us how to say good-bye to Abby ourselves. Guess what? We already knew it all along. You do, too — it's just a wave!

Momma and I walk out to the van. "Now I really am on my way to being a gymnastics queen!" I squeal. "But first I have to learn enough to participate in the Gold Star Showcase event."

"We'll talk to your new coach tomorrow," Momma tells me. "Then we'll find out all about the showcase."

Chapter Four
Lesson One

"Yay!" I say as we pull away.

On Tuesday morning, Ugly Brother helps
me pick out the perfect outfit for my very first
gymnastics lesson. We finally decide on pink
shorts and a pink T-shirt with a big gold star on
the front. When I come downstairs for breakfast,
I twirl around.

Momma is impressed! "A gold star outfit for a
gold star gym," says Momma.

"Yes, ma'am!" I shout.

We eat a very quick breakfast of eggs and biscuits. I don't want to be too full or too late for my first lesson! Beginner lessons start at nine o'clock sharp. When we have finished eating, I clear the table and put the dishes in the sink. I am doing extra chores to earn money for my lessons. They are worth it!

Momma says, "Thank you, Kylie Jean. Good job!"

We head out the door, get into the van, and start driving to the gymnastics center. On the way, I borrow Momma's cell phone. I want to look up how to say *friend* in sign language. After a few clicks, I find it. I can't wait to show Abby that I know how to say *friend*!

"Be good, and do what your coach asks of you!" Momma tells me. "I'll be back to pick you up in an hour."

"Yes, Momma," I answer.

Inside, I see Abby with another class. She smiles and does a back handspring.

The nice lady at the front desk tells me that my lesson is with Coach Amanda. "The beginner classes meet on the blue mat," she says.

"Yes, ma'am," I say, "and thank you!"

I walk out to the mat. Coach Amanda is sitting there with four girls. "Are you new?" she asks.

I am about to answer, when in walks a girl who is almost late. You'll never guess who it is! It's Paula Dupree! Paula and I laugh and hug.

Yes, I am new, and so is Paula," I answer, pointing to my friend. "My name is Kylie Jean."

"Welcome to our beginner class! You girls can come over and sit on the mat with the rest of our class," Coach Amanda says as she pats the mat with her hand.

We have six girls in the beginner class. We all sit in a big circle on the mat. Paula and I sit next to each other.

Coach Amanda says, "Why don't the rest of you all say your names, too? That way we will all know each other."

The other girls in our class are Sissy, Monica, Belle, and Ella Rose. Ella Rose has two names, just like me!

Coach says, "Before we do gymnastics, we always have to stretch. It prepares our muscles for the hard work we'll be doing. I like to start with the basics, so let's work on a forward roll."

She models the perfect forward roll for us. One by one, we all roll down the mat. We look like donuts rolling off a tray. Coach has us practice the forward roll several times.

"Practice makes perfect," she says, "right?"

We all shout, "Right!"

My momma says that, too. All athletes have to practice. My brother, T.J., has practice all the time. I bet Courtney Bell practices every single day to be good enough to win a gold medal.

"Can anyone do a cartwheel?" asks Coach.

Paula raises her hand.

"Paula, would you like to show the girls a cartwheel?" asks Coach.

"Sure," answers Paula. She starts on her feet, then she leans over onto her hands. She keeps moving quickly like a wheel, until she lands on her feet again.

We all cheer and clap for Paula. Coach does a cartwheel in slow motion, making sure we know where to put our hands when we start. Then we all try, one at a time. Coach Amanda spots us. That means she stands close by to help us if we start to fall. No one falls, though, because we are all careful.

Paula whispers, "We're not even doing the hard stuff yet."

I giggle, "I know, we're not ready for that yet."

"Who can do the splits?" Coach asks.

I shout, "Me! I can!"

I show everyone how I do the splits. All the girls try it. Some can do it the first time they try it. Others struggle.

Coach suggests we do stretching exercises to improve our flexibility. We all practice. Ella Rose is good at doing the splits, just like me!

Then the owner of the Gold Star Gymnastics Center, Miss Becky, calls all of the classes over for a big announcement. Everyone gathers around. I get to stand by Abby.

"Soon we are going to have a huge Gymnastics Showcase to get folks interested in the sport," says Miss Becky. "It will be held a week from Saturday. Everyone can participate!"

We are all so excited! We jump and tumble and cheer. I bump into Paula, and we laugh. I explain to Paula that Abby can't hear.

I have a surprise for Abby. Pointing to Paula, I lock my pointer fingers first one way and then the other to show that Paula is my friend. Abby starts signing really fast, her hands flying. I shake my head to show that I don't understand. She looks around, right and left. Then she sees her momma and waves for her to come over.

Mrs. Golden watches Abby signing, then she turns to me and says, "Abby is wondering if you are learning sign language."

I say, "No, ma'am. Really, I just looked up the word *friend* on the Internet."

Mrs. Golden says, "Not many girls can speak to Abby in sign language. That was very thoughtful of you, Kylie Jean!"

Abby smiles and touches her hand to her mouth. Then she extends her arm out in front of her.

Mrs. Golden says, "Abby is saying—"

"Thank you!" I jump in.

"That's right!" Mrs. Golden says. "Remember, Abby can read lips, too. If you talk slowly and face her, she can understand what you are saying."

I am thinking I should learn both gymnastics and sign language! When I get home, I'm going to do an Internet search on learning American Sign Language.

Coach calls us back to the blue mat. I wave good-bye to Abby. Coach asks if anyone wants to perform in the showcase. My hand shoots right up.

"Yay for Kylie Jean!" Coach says. "I love your energy. Anyone else?"

No one else raises her hand.

"Well, it looks like you'll be going solo, Kylie Jean," Coach says. "Start working on your routine, and we'll talk again at your next lesson. You're going to be awesome! Let's give Kylie Jean a round of applause for representing our class!"

Everyone claps. Paula claps the loudest. I stand and spread my arms like a swan, just like Courtney Bell did, and then I take a bow.

Just then, Momma walks up. "Time to go, sugar," she says.

"I have so much to tell you!" I reply. "I'm going to be in the showcase. I found out all about it. I made some new friends! One has two names like me. Today we did forward rolls, cartwheels, and splits. I got to show everyone how to do the splits. Also, can we go to the library? I need to get a special book."

Chapter Five
Practice Makes Perfect

I spend the next day thinking about my routine. I have only ten days to practice before the big gymnastics showcase!

My first idea for the showcase is a balance beam routine. It will be perfect for me, since I will be performing solo. The balance beam is totally new for me, but Courtney Bell made it look pretty easy. Over ham and cheese sandwiches, I tell Momma about my idea.

"You'd better practice first," she warns. "I'll bet it's harder than it looks."

"I know, Momma," I reply. "But I need Daddy to help me with one little thing when he gets home."

Momma asks, "Can I help?"

"Yes," I answer, "but we'll need Daddy, too."

Momma nods. The potato chips in my mouth go *CRUNCH, CRUNCH, CRUNCH*. Ugly Brother whines because he wants some, too. He loves chips! I give him a few, but he doesn't crunch them. Instead, he swallows them without even chewing. Silly doggie!

All afternoon Momma watches the Olympics. I don't want to watch because I am busy learning gymnastics and sign language.

Ugly Brother and I go upstairs to read. I sit on my bed reading my special library book, *Sign Language for Beginners*. My doggie brother takes a nap. The clock by the bed seems to be broken because the hands move slower than a turtle in tall grass. I read, I watch the clock, I wait. Finally the door to Daddy's truck bangs shut in the driveway. I run down the stairs lickety-split with Ugly Brother right behind me.

Daddy shouts, "Hello, anyone home?"

"Me! I'm home," I yell.

Daddy and I share a big squeezy hug. "What have you been up to?" Daddy asks.

Before he can put down his briefcase, I reply, "I'm working on a plan, and I need your help!"

"What's up, buttercup?" Daddy asks.

"I really need to borrow an old landscape timber from the garage to use as a practice balance beam," I reply.

Daddy smiles. "All right, then," he says. "Let's get you set up in the backyard."

Ugly Brother and I watch while Daddy and Momma move the timber to the backyard and set it down in the soft grass.

"Is it ready?" I ask.

"Yes, it is," Daddy says. "Are you ready?"

"I guess we'll see, because I'm going to try out this beam!" I say.

Daddy and Momma walk over to the deck. They sit down to watch me pratice on my new balance beam. It is finally cooling down outside.

Carefully, I try to walk and turn gracefully on
the beam. I try to stay on my toes, using my arms
to help me balance. It's tricky, but I won't give
up yet. Momma always says, "Practice makes
perfect!"

Ugly Brother tries next. He is not graceful at all! He slips around like a pig in mud. I must admit, I wiggle and wobble quite a bit, too. Unfortunately, I can't walk backward or on my tippy toes without falling off the beam. This is much harder than it looks on TV!

T.J. joins our parents on the deck. He begs, "Lil' Bit, please stop. I can't look! You're going to twist your ankle, I just know it!"

"Maybe you're right," I reply. "I don't have enough balance for the balance beam after all. But Carters are not quitters, so I will just have to think of another event that I can do. Besides, Coach Amanda is counting on me to represent our class. The other girls are too scared or shy."

"That's the spirit!" says Daddy. "I know you'll come up with something fantastic."

Momma says, "You still have time. Maybe your coach can help you."

Every day for the rest of the week, I go to lessons at Gold Star with Coach Amanda. On Thursday, I see Paula there, and I have something really important to tell her. I run over to meet her on a blue mat.

"My solo idea is not working out very well. No matter what I do, it doesn't seem very exciting."

"I know what you mean," Paula agrees. "Making it fun is harder than it looks."

Just then, we see Abby Golden. She's stretching out on a mat that's across the gym from us.

"I have a secret surprise for Abby!" I tell Paula. "I have been practicing sign language, too. Each afternoon, I work on spelling out the alphabet with my hands. I can already spell K-Y-L-I-E."

"Now that's exciting!" Paula replies. "You are a really good friend!"

* * *

On Friday, Coach Amanda has Abby demonstrate tumbling for the beginner class. When she finishes, we all clap and cheer.

Abby takes a bow and says *thank you* in sign language.

I make a sign like a sliding scoop, and Abby's eyes pop open wide. She knows I have learned another word. It is *welcome*, as in *you are welcome*. I smile, and Abby smiles back.

Paula turns to me and says, "Hey, I have an idea. Maybe we can do a routine together — a partner routine!"

Abby gives us a thumbs-up and waves her momma over. She has been reading our lips and has a good suggestion. She thinks that since we are beginners, we should focus on moves we know.

It's a fabulous idea, so we ask Coach Amanda for help.

Coach teaches us two more moves to add to our routine. First, we learn how to do a bridge. It's kind of tricky. We lie on our backs on the floor and push our stomachs up toward the ceiling. I like the next move, the back bend, much better. We start standing up and bend backward until we can touch the floor with our hands.

Coach Amanda joins us. She stands next to me
and quickly does a back bend. We are two bridges
next to each other! With all my new moves, I
feel like I am learning how to be a real, true
gymnastics queen!

Chapter Six
Friends on the Floor

On Monday, with only five days left until the big showcase, Paula and I have decided to go ahead with Abby's suggestion to do a partner floor routine with moves we already know. I have been watching Courtney Bell's Olympic routine all afternoon.

"Momma, I've been trying to get ideas for a partner routine by watching gymnastics, but I still don't have any," I complain.

"Why don't you call Paula and see if she has any more ideas?" Momma suggests.

I find Paula's number and give her a call. *Ring . . . ring . . . ring.* A voice answers. It's Paula's momma.

"May I please speak with Paula?" I ask.

Pretty soon, my friend takes the phone. "Hi, Kylie Jean," she says.

"Hi, Paula!" I say. "I've been thinking about our showcase routine. Courtney Bell is a champion, and her routine is too hard for a beginner. But like Courtney, I know we will need music. Also, some of her moves, like leaps and split leaps, don't look too hard."

"Okay," Paula says. "Let's ask Coach to help with leaps tomorrow."

"Maybe our friend Abby can help, too," I add.

Paula says, "See you tomorrow!"

"Right!" I say. "Bye for now."

The next day at Gold Star, the first thing we do is look for our coach. We both see her at the same time, and we run over.

"Coach, can you pretty please help us?" Paula asks. "We have some ideas for our floor routine, but we would like to learn how to do leaps and split leaps."

"Can you show us how to do them?" I ask.

"Sure!" Coach answers. "Those moves are pretty easy, so once I get the other beginner girls going, let's have a little mini lesson."

"Hooray!" we shout.

While everyone else is practicing simple rolls on the blue mat, Coach takes us over to the red mat. "Leaps take a lot of room," she says. "You'll need a whole mat to work on."

First we stretch on the mat, warming up. Coach stretches with us. Then she asks us to watch while she does a leap and a split leap.

I whisper, "Those leaps are perfect — just like the ones Courtney Bell did!"

Paula wants to go first. She gets a running start, and then she tries a leap and a split leap, just like Coach.

"Pretty good!" Coach shouts. "Remember to be careful when landing. Now it's your turn, Kylie Jean."

I take a few steps and then leap into the air, picturing the perfect leap and split leap in my head. But my legs feel heavy, like I have muddy boots on my feet.

"Kylie, that was fine, but you should point your toes," says Coach. "Just think splits, but in the air. You both stay here and practice while I go help Belle."

I need to practice more! While we practice, Paula and I talk about our routine. Paula wants to do her cartwheel.

Soon, Abby comes over to the mat to see what we are doing. Her momma joins us. Abby wants us to know that our routine should be about a minute and a half long. I touch my lips twice with an open flat hand to say thank you. Abby smiles excitedly and does the same.

Her momma says, "Kylie Jean, you are getting better and better at signing."

"She's teaching me a little, too!" says Paula.

Mrs. Golden asks, "Do you know what you want to do for your routine?"

"Well, I think we should start our routine by holding hands," says Paula. "That will show that we are best friends. What do y'all think?"

Mrs. Golden, Abby, and I all like the idea a lot. When Coach comes over to check on us, she has a plan, too. She wants us to keep working on the red mat while we come up with more ideas for our floor program. As Abby and her momma watch, we try different starting moves. Finally, we decide that a leap is definitely the easiest thing to do while holding hands.

I ask, "What should we do next?"

Paula replies, "Well, we have to let go when we land."

"You're right," I reply. "What if we both do a kick?"

We decide to try it. We leap, land, and drop each other's hands. Then we both do a kick.

Mrs. Golden says, "Good job, girls. It looks nice, so far."

Abby nods and gives us a thumbs-up.

Paula says, "I want to do my cartwheel next."

Coach Amanda has been going back and forth from our mat to the blue mat. She gives us some more advice. "I think you should save your special move until the very end for the grand finale."

Paula and I agree, so instead we both do a forward roll. To make sure everything flows together, we start again from the beginning. For our next move, Abby thinks we should raise our arms into the air and do a jump full turn. Then we do a handstand followed by a back bend. Abby does the moves with us.

"That's a lot of moves!" I say.

Only an advanced student like Abby could think of such an awesome set of moves.

Once again, we start from the very beginning. Mrs. Golden times us with her watch. "It's been 82 seconds!" she warns. "You girls have time for only one more move."

Paula and I give each other a high five. Finally, it's time to add our special signature move. Paula will do her cartwheel, and I will do the splits. The last thing we do is stand up and extend our arms like swan wings, just like Courtney Bell.

Mrs. Golden and Abby clap loudly. I smile, but then I see that Momma is here to pick me up!

"Can we please stay a little longer?" I ask.

Momma replies, "Yes, we have a little time."

"Guess what?" I say. "Our routine is finally finished and we want to show everyone!"

We run through the whole routine. At the very end I can't resist giving a little beauty queen wave, nice and slow, side-to-side.

Paula shouts, "Ta-da!"

Everyone cheers.

"That was terrific!" Momma says. "You have learned a lot in just a few days."

"These girls are really motivated," says Coach.

Paula and I smile at each other. Now we have only three days until the rehearsal. We need music and leotards!

Chapter Seven

Lollipop

At dinner that night, I am tickled pink to announce that Paula and I finally have our routine ready.

"They just need music and leotards," Momma adds.

T.J. laughs and says, "I think leotards are weird and funny."

"What's the big deal? A leotard is just like a one-piece bathing suit."

"Why can't you wear pants with it?" T.J. asks.

I shrug because I don't even know the answer to that.

Momma is already thinking of some music for our routine. She suggests that we choose some fun, upbeat music. Everyone starts talking at the same time, making suggestions.

Daddy likes a pop song called "Lollipop." T.J. starts singing a popular song he knows. But Momma thinks we should pick something else.

When we are done eating, I have to clear the table before I can call Paula. While I take the dishes into the kitchen, Daddy plays his song for me. It's really good and has lots of energy. I think we've found the perfect song!

I quickly call Paula to tell her about the song.

The phone rings only one time before Paula picks it up.

"Hey, I was hoping you would call," Paula says. "Did you think of anything for us to wear or a song we can use?"

"I didn't, but my daddy thought of a song!" I reply. "It's called 'Lollipop.'" Have you heard of the song?"

"I haven't heard of that one," she says. Can you play it? I would like to listen to it, too."

I call for Daddy to start the song over again. Then I hold the phone close to the speaker so Paula can hear the music. I let the whole song play for her, and then I put the phone back up to my ear.

"Do you like it?" I ask.

Paula is super excited. "I LOVE it!" she says.
"I especially like the name. How about wearing
pretty candy-striped bows with pink leotards?"

"I LOVE that idea!" I reply. "We make a great
team!"

"We will need your momma and granny to help us make the bows," says Paula. "Can they help with that?"

I tell Paula that I will ask Momma, but I am sure they can help us. Then we say good-bye and hang up.

Before I go to bed, I want to practice sign language. I am learning how to sign *good night*. First I say it out loud. Then I show Ugly Brother *good night* in sign language. I bend my elbow and hold my arm straight in front of my stomach. Then I touch my chin with my right fingertips, flip my palm away from me, and then cup it over my left hand. It looks just like a low moon over the ground. I make the motion over and over again. Ugly Brother is watching, but he is not used to sign language.

"Do you understand *good night*?" I ask.

He barks, "Ruff, ruff."

That means he does. Momma comes in to say it's almost bedtime. We have been practicing for a while!

"Please can we stay up longer?" I beg.

Momma pulls back my curtain. There is no moonlight. It's darker than the inside of a pocket!

Momma suggests, "How about a bubble bath and then bedtime?"

"Okay," I agree. A bubble bath sounds fun, even if bedtime doesn't. Besides, Ugly Brother loves a bubble bath! He always chases bubbles around the bathroom while I soak in the tub. Before we know it, I'm squeaky clean, in my PJs, and ready for prayers and a good night kiss. When Momma comes in, I make the sign for *good night*.

"Kylie Jean, I'm impressed that you are working so hard on learning two new things at once!" she says. "Abby is going to be so happy and surprised when she finds out you can speak her language."

"Thank you, Momma," I say.

I settle in, as snug as a bug in a rug. Ugly Brother is snoring away before I can even close my eyes.

* * *

In the morning, I have a few questions for Momma. "Can you and Granny help us make some hair bows to wear with our leotards?" I ask. "And after my lesson today, can we buy a pink leotard at the gymnastics center shop? Paula wants to get one, too. It's important that the two of us match for our big performance."

Momma replies, "Sure thing, sugar! I'll call Granny while you're at your lesson and ask if she can help. After your lesson, we'll take a look in the shop for leotards."

Momma drives me to my lesson. At the center, Paula shows Abby and me a picture she drew of the hair bow she has in mind.

"Oh, I love it!" I gush.

Abby gives it two thumbs up!

"I'm glad y'all like it," Paula says. "It's really big and will stand out!"

"Can I take it to show my granny?" I ask.

"Sure!" Paula replies. "Do you think she can make one like my picture?"

"Yup!" I say. "Granny can make almost anything!"

We practice our routine while Abby goes to work on the uneven bars. The bars look kind of scary, but I know we'll soon be ready to try them out!

After our lesson, Paula and I meet our mommas near the front desk.

"Please, can we go look at leotards in the gym shop?" we ask them.

Luckily, the mommas agree, so we walk into the shop. Leotards are even on sale! A sign says "Buy One, Get One Free" in big pink letters. Paula and I spot the perfect pink leotards for our showcase routine.

"Momma, can we please get this one?" asks Paula.

Momma turns to Paula's momma. "Would you want to split the cost?" she asks.

"Sure! I love a good deal!" says Paula's momma.

Paula and I grin as we watch our mommas pay for the leotards. Then we say good-bye. I wave good-bye to Abby, too, but she is swinging high up on the bars and can't wave back.

When we get to the van, I ask, "Can we stop by Granny's house on the way home?"

Momma says, "Yes, I think we can do that."

"Can I help make the bows?" I ask.

"We'll see," Momma replies. "Let's ask Granny when we get there."

Granny gives me a big squeezy hug when we arrive. "I've sure been missing you!" she squeals.

"Kylie Jean has been busy with gymnastics lessons," Momma says. "She wants to be a gymnastics queen!"

"I never met a girl with more determination," Granny says. "You can do anything you set your mind to."

I tell her all about our routine, our leotards, and the gymnastics showcase. Then I tell Granny that we really need her help.

"You know I'd do anything for you, sweet girl!" says Granny.

I show Granny the picture of the pretty pink bow that Paula drew.

"Making that bow will be as easy as pie!" Granny says. "I know just what to do."

"Can I help?" I ask.

We go to her craft room, where she has lots of colorful ribbon.

"You can help me pick the perfect ribbon," she says.

Holding some up, I ask, "How about this glittery striped ribbon? It has all different shades of pink, from soft cotton candy pink to bright bubble gum pink!"

"Perfect!" says Granny.

She twists and twists layers of the ribbon into bows. Momma attaches them to silver hair clips. When they are finished, the bows look perfect!

"Thank you, Granny and Momma," I say. "The bows are wonderful!"

Now, it's my turn to give Granny a big squeezy hug!

Chapter Eight
Rehearsal

I wake up, rub my eyes, and stretch sleepily.
Then I realize it's Friday. We've been practicing
all week, and today is the day of our official
rehearsal. It's this evening at six o'clock sharp.
Everyone must attend, and no one can be late!
If someone is late, she can't perform in the show.

For now, I need to get ready for my lesson at the
gym. Paula and I want to practice some more!

After breakfast, Momma drops me off at the gymnastics center. I bring a CD with our special song on it.

Inside the gym, everyone is hard at work. I see Abby by the uneven bars, and I sign *hello*. She signs *hello* back. Paula is already on the red mat walking through our routine.

"Finally!" Paula says. "I was getting worried that you might not come."

"I'm not late!" I say. "I think you're a bit early."

Soon, Coach Amanda walks over to us and says, "Let's practice, girls!"

The other girls want to watch us. Ella Rose, Sissy, Monica, and Belle sit cross-legged by the edge of the mat.

Paula and I take our places on the mat holding hands. When the music begins, we both start moving. We run through our entire routine without missing a single step! Our friends cheer.

Later, Paula's momma comes to drive us home. That's when I reveal my special plan for the afternoon.

"Can Paula come over to my house and work on our routine?" I ask.

"Can I?" Paula adds. "I'll be good!"

Her momma agrees, and before you know it, we are in my backyard. Paula and I use duct tape to mark off a mat-sized square on the grass. Ugly Brother tries to help, but the tape sticks to his nose. He wiggles around trying to loosen the tape. His side of the square ends up looking squiggly.

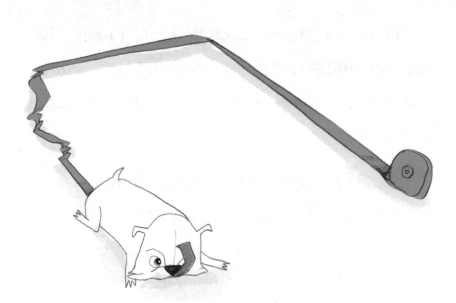

"Sorry, Ugly Brother," I say. "We're going to have to redo your side, but don't feel bad. I have another job for you!"

He barks, "Ruff, ruff."

"You can help us practice, and then I'll teach you how to do a forward roll," I say.

"Are you sure he can help us?" asks Paula.

"I have a really good job for him," I reply. "Just you wait and see. We'll practice, and Ugly Brother can give us a score. I even made him some scoring papers. See?"

I hold up a stack of papers with numbers on them. I made them all 10s, because we want to be perfect! I show them to Ugly Brother and explain his job. He will hold them up to let us know how we are doing. If we do a perfect job, he holds the paper in his teeth, running around in a circle. If we make a mistake, he can bark.

The first time we go through the routine, I forget to do my kick. Ugly Brother jumps up and down barking. I promise Paula that next time I'll do better. After that, we do our routine perfectly so many times that the score sheet is all wet from all the doggie drool.

We decide to run through it one more time. When we're done, we decide to teach Ugly Brother some gymnastics moves. Paula and I show him the forward roll, but he does it sideways. He rolls and rolls.

Paula whispers, "I don't think he is doing it right."

"He can't go forward, but he's having fun anyway!" I whisper back.

"Ugly Brother, you're doing such a great job," I tell him. "You can be a gymnastics king!"

He barks excitedly, "Ruff, ruff."

Then it's time for Paula to go home and get ready for the rehearsal.

Later that afternoon, we arrive at the gymnastics center. It's full of gymnasts doing all sorts of wonderful moves. One girl swings completely around the highest bar. It's Abby! She dismounts with a twisting flip and lands perfectly on the mat.

"That looks really hard to do," says Paula.

"Well, we aren't ready for that yet," I say. "That's why we're beginners, but we'll learn!"

Coach calls us over to practice our routine. When we finish, she is so happy with our performance.

"Awesome!" she says. "You two have done an amazing job learning a floor routine in such a short amount of time. Your leotards and bows are super cute, too!"

"Thanks!" we reply.

Coach adds, "You are READY for the showcase!"

Chapter Nine
Showcase Showtime

Finally, it's the day of the big Gold Star Gymnastics Center Showcase! I'm ready, but I have nervous butterflies in my stomach. Everyone is coming to see me perform. Momma, Daddy, T.J., Ugly Brother, Granny, Pappy, Nanny, and Pa will all be there.

I get dressed in my pink leotard. Momma fixes my hair in a ponytail with the big pink candy-striped bow.

At breakfast, Daddy says I look sweet from my head to the tips of my glittery pink flip-flops.

"Are those tumbling flip-flops?" Daddy teases.

"No, Daddy!" I say. "Gymnasts don't need shoes. We do better without them, so I'll take them off to perform."

He laughs and winks at me. Then he gives me a surprise — two beautiful, giant, tasty pink lollipops! They are as big as saucers.

He says, "Your momma thinks you should hold them up at the end of your routine."

"Thank you, thank you, Daddy!" I reply.

"After the showcase, you can eat them as a treat!" he adds.

"Yay, and YUMMY!" I shout.

Everyone piles into the van, even Ugly Brother. Gold Star is expecting so many people to come that there are extra places to park in the field beside the gym. When we arrive, it's already getting crowded, and we have to park in the field.

Inside, the gym is set up with several floor mats, balance beams, uneven bars, and some vaulting horses. I will have to remember to tease Pa about those horses, because they're not like the ones he's used to. I finally spy Paula and Abby by Coach Amanda. I run over to join them.

Abby gives us a thumbs-up and heads to her place by the bars.

I slip the lollipops out of my bag. "What if we hold these up at the end of our routine?" I ask.

"Yes!" she says. "They're fun."

The showcase is starting! We lock our pinkies together and wait until it is our turn to perform. We watch Abby sail through the air during her routine. She sticks it. That's gymnastics talk for performing a perfect routine.

It's time!

Paula whispers, "I'm nervous."

"Me too," I whisper, "but we're ready! We have practiced, and Momma always tells me that practice makes perfect."

Paula nods. We step out onto the mat. I find my spot. Out of the corner of my eye, I see Coach Amanda giving us a thumbs-up. Then I see my family and grandparents. They are smiling and waving. I give them a quick beauty queen wave. Paula and I take our places, holding hands. I wink at my friend.

"Ready?" I whisper.

"Yeah!" she says.

The music starts, and we leap! At first I am trying hard to think about my routine. I want every move to be perfect, but then suddenly, I'm not thinking anymore. I'm just doing it! We kick, do a jump full turn, a forward roll, handstand, and a back bend.

Then we pause.

I look at Paula, and we smile at each other. I do the splits while Paula does her cartwheel. We finish with a flourish by picking up the lollipops at the edge of the mat and holding them high.

The crowd claps and cheers!

We run over to Coach Amanda and Abby. I am so thankful to my new friend for helping me! I can't wait to show her my surprise. Starting with my hand on my lips, I say *thank you* and then spell out Abby's name in sign language. Abby blinks. She asks me if I have learned how to sign. It takes me a while to understand, but then I nod. Abby gives me a big squeezy hug. She is so excited and happy!

Guess what? I just found out there's only one thing better than being a gymnastics queen, and that's making a new friend!

Marci Bales Peschke was born in Indiana, grew up in Florida, and now lives in Texas with her husband, two children, and a feisty black-and-white cat named Phoebe. She loves reading and watching movies.

When **Tuesday Mourning** was a little girl, she knew she wanted to be an artist when she grew up. Now, she is an illustrator who lives in Utah. She especially loves illustrating books for kids and teenagers. When she isn't illustrating, Tuesday loves spending time with her husband, who is an actor, and their two sons and one daughter.

Glossary

advanced (ad-VANSED)—more difficult or demanding

choreograph (KOR-ee-uh-graf)—to create and arrange movements that make up a routine

dismount (DIS-mount)—a move done to get off an apparatus

flourish (FLUR-ish)—to develop and succeed

hesitate (HEZ-i-tate)—to pause before saying or doing something, especially because you feel nervous or unsure

participate (pahr-TIS-uh-pate)—to join with others in an activity or event

rehearsal (ri-HUR-suhl)—a practice, especially for a performance

routine (roo-TEEN)—a performance that is practiced repeatedly to be performed

showcase (SHOH-kase)—to display something or someone boldly

sign language (SINE LANG-gwij)—hand signs that stand for words, letters, and numbers

split leap (SPLIT LEEP)—a jump up with your legs spread out in opposite directions

Talk!

1. Lots of people help Kylie Jean in this book. Who would you go to if you needed help with something? Talk about your answer.

2. Kylie Jean meets a new friend in the beginning of this book. How does Kylie reach out to her new friend? Is there someone you could reach out to as a new friend? What are some ways you could reach out to that person?

3. What do you think happens after this story ends? Talk about it!

Be Creative!

1. Kylie Jean's goal is to be a gymnastics queen. What's your number-one dream?

2. Who is your favorite character in this story? Draw a picture of that person. Then write a list of five things you know about him or her.

3. Learning new activities can be fun. Write about an activity you'd like to learn and why.

This is the perfect treat for any Gymnastics Queen!
Just make sure to ask a grown-up for help.

Love, Kylie Jean

From Momma's Kitchen

STRAWBERRY LOLLIPOPS

YOU NEED:

- oil spray
- lollipop molds and sticks
- 1 cup sugar
- 1/3 cup corn syrup
- 1/2 cup water
- 1/4 cup cream
- 1 teaspoon strawberry syrup
- red liquid food coloring
- a grown-up helper

1. Spray a cookie sheet with oil.

2. Spray lollipop molds with oil. Then place a lollipop stick in each mold. Place molds on the cookie sheet.

3. In a saucepan over medium heat, stir together sugar, corn syrup, water, and cream until all sugar dissolves. Stop stirring when mixture begins to boil.

4. Ask an adult to place a candy thermometer in the pan to make sure the mixture reaches 300°F.

5. Remove pan from heat and let cool to 270°F. Stir in syrup and food coloring.

6. Pour mixture into molds. Let cool for 10 minutes.

Yum, yum!